333: The Truck with a Big Heart

By Edward W. Venning
Illustrated By Risa Horiuchi

Outskirts Press, Inc.
Denver, Colorado

Outskirts Press
http://www.outskirtspress.com

ISBN-13: 978-1-4327-0738-5

Outskirts Press and the "OP" logo are trademarks belonging to
Outskirts Press, Inc.

Printed in the United States of America

Thanks To

Donna Venning; Don Merlino and the family at Stoneway Concrete – EV

Mom, Dad and Rina; Mark Livingston; Kevin Perrine – RH

Special thanks to my son, Kevin Edward Venning -- EV

Some dads work in offices with computers, some dads work in classrooms teaching kids. Other dads go to work in big office buildings and still other dads are police officers or firemen.

Kevin's dad, Richard, drove a big concrete mixer for Stone Concrete.

Sometimes Kevin would go to work with his dad and sit in the cab of the truck and pretend to drive.   Kevin loved to see the big, gray drum go round and round and watch his dad control the buttons and barrels that poured the cement.

Kevin dreamt of the day that he would be able to help his dad and maybe even drive the truck himself.

Kevin grew up and decided to work for Stone Concrete, so his dad introduced him to the boss, Marty. Marty liked Richard and all the hard work he had done so he gave Kevin a job driving, too.

Marty gave Kevin the same truck his father had driven for many years, Truck 335.   The truck was old but had a lot of heart. Marty told Kevin if he took care of the truck, she would take care of him, too.

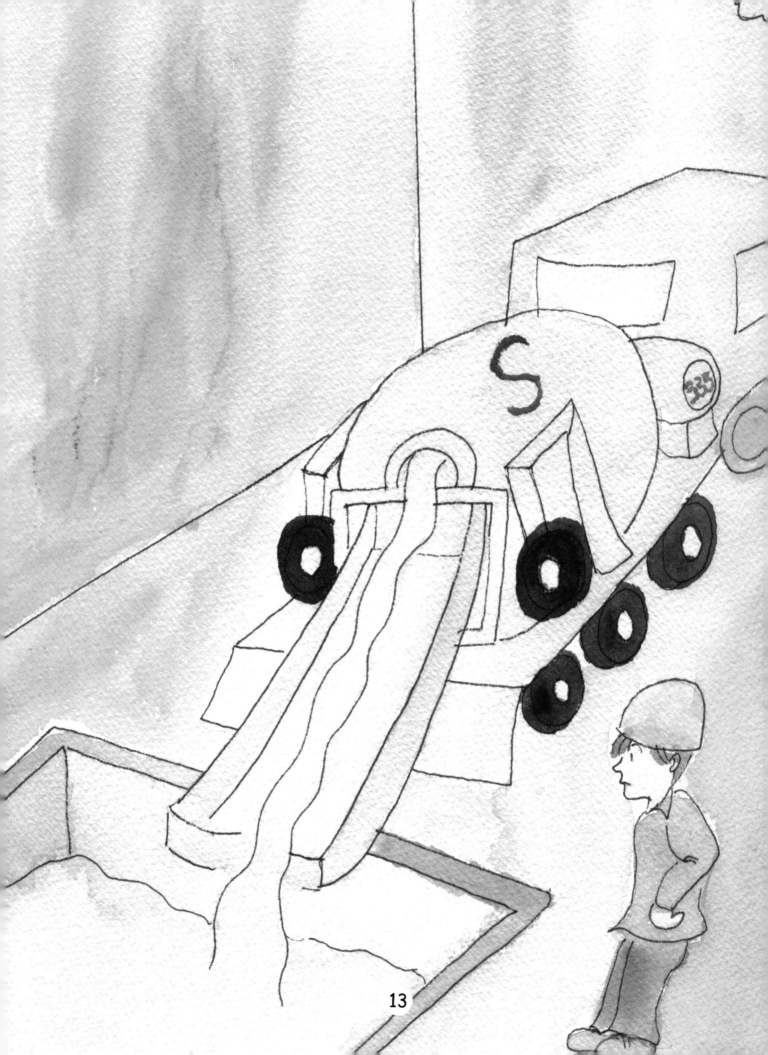

Because Kevin was a new driver, Marty didn't send Kevin to any big construction jobs like the huge football stadium or the new train depot. Kevin and Truck 335 were sent to small jobs, pouring concrete for house foundations, basketball courts and sidewalks. Kevin never complained; he just worked hard and took care of Truck 335.

When the other drivers would brag about the tall skyscraper or the gigantic new grocery store they were working on, Kevin would just smile and be happy for them. Then he would turn his attention back to Truck 335.

He would clean and polish her and always drove very carefully so that no one would be hurt by the truck. And just like Marty had told him, Truck 335 started to take care of Kevin.

She never broke down on the side of the road or got a flat tire. Even when she was very tired, she always got Kevin to the jobsite on time...in rain, in snow or in the scorching hot sun. Truck 335 was always dependable.

The other trucks didn't like Truck 335.

She was old and had wheels that went under the truck instead of over the top like the new trucks. Her engine was big and loud, while the new trucks had smaller, quiet engines.

She was the oldest in the fleet and the other trucks thought she should just retire.

But Truck 335 had the biggest heart of all the trucks.

29

Kevin and Truck 335 started to work very well together.   Marty was happy with the team and started to send them on big jobs like the other trucks.

Most of the other trucks were jealous of the team, but Kevin and Truck 335 kept working hard to be the best and safest team on the road.

Because Kevin took such good care of Truck 335, Marty decided to give Kevin a new truck.

Truck 335 was sad because she had come to depend on Kevin.

Even though Kevin's new truck was easier to drive because of its small engine, Kevin always felt strange driving it.

Marty saw this, so he told Kevin instead of a brand new truck, they would put a new engine in Truck 335, and new wheels that went up over the top of the truck. Plus, they gave her a beautiful, new paint job.

Truck 335 loved the new changes......

...and Kevin loved it because he had a "new" truck with the same heart.

Printed in the United States
91105LV00001BA